RICHARD SCARRY'S
Great Big Schoolhouse
Readers

One, Two, AH-CHOO!

Illustrated by Huck Scarry
Written by Erica Farber

STERLING CHILDREN'S BOOKS
New York

Sally Cat had a cold.
One, two, AH-CHOO!

Huckle played games with her.
Lowly played games with her.

Wow! Look at all the toys!

Mrs. Cat had a cold.

One, two, AH-CHOO!

Lowly made toast for her.

Huckle got juice for her.

OOPS! The tray fell.

The boys fell.

One, two, AH-CHOO!

Mr. Cat sneezed.

Oh, no! No more tissues!

Huckle and Lowly went to
the store. There was Ella.
One, two, AH-CHOO!
Ella sneezed.
She dropped an orange.

Huckle picked up the orange.
CRASH! There went the oranges!

When they got home,
there was Bridget.
One, two, AH-CHOO!
Bridget sneezed.

"Here is a tissue," said Huckle.

He did not see the wheelbarrow.
OOPS!

It was time for school.

Huckle and Lowly ran for the bus.

One, two, AH-CHOO!

Arthur sneezed.

He dropped his backpack.

His stuff fell out.

Huckle and Lowly picked up
his stuff.
"I have a cold," said Arthur.
"I am going home."

At school, Molly sneezed.
One, two, AH-CHOO!

She sneezed again.
One, two, AH-CHOO!

So, Huckle and Lowly took
Molly to the nurse.

13

One, two, AH-CHOO!

Frances sneezed.

Frances had a cold, too.

So, Huckle and Lowly took Frances
to the nurse.

Huckle, Lowly, and Skip played tag.
One, two, AH-CHOO! Skip sneezed.

Skip had a cold.
He took himself to the nurse.

Huckle and Lowly looked at Miss Honey. They were the only ones left at school.

So, Huckle and Lowly made get-well cards.

One, two, AH-CHOO!
Miss Honey sneezed.
Huckle and Lowly made her
a get-well card, too.

Huckle and Lowly took a
get-well card to Ella.

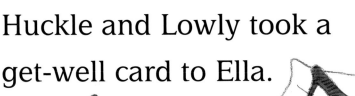

They took one to Arthur
and one to Molly.

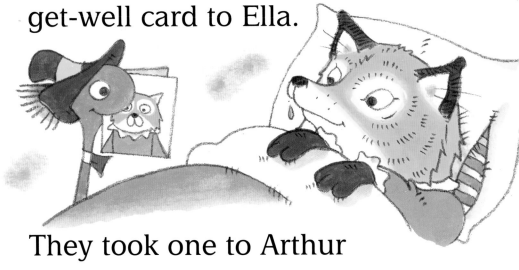

They took one to Frances…

…one to Skip…

…and one to Bridget.

Thank you, Huckle and Lowly!

Then Huckle and Lowly went home. One, two, AH-CHOO! Huckle and Lowly sneezed.

Huckle and Lowly had colds, too.

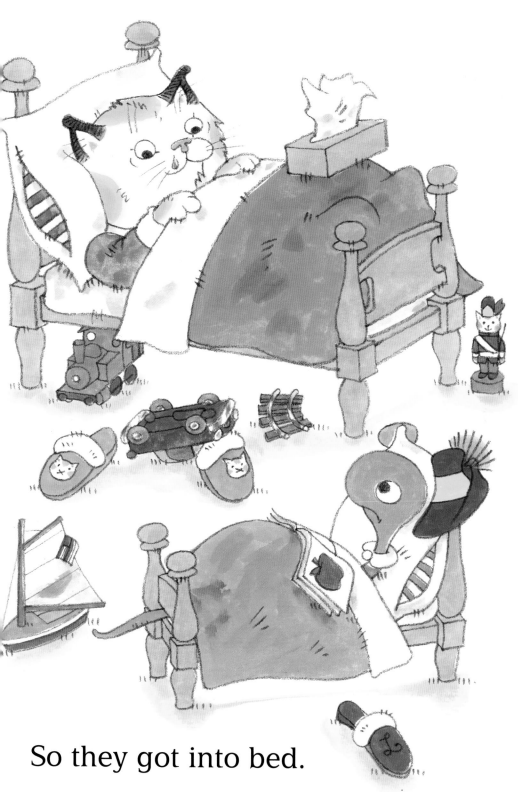

So they got into bed.

Sally played games with them.
Mrs. Cat got toast and juice
for them.

Mr. Cat got tissues for them.

One, two, AH-CHOO!

STERLING CHILDREN'S BOOKS
New York

An Imprint of Sterling Publishing
387 Park Avenue South
New York, NY 10016

STERLING CHILDREN'S BOOKS and the distinctive Sterling Children's Books logo
are registered trademarks of Sterling Publishing Co., Inc.

Text © 2013 by JB Publishing, Inc.
Illustrations © 2013 by Richard Scarry Corporation
All characters are the property of the Richard Scarry Corporation.

ISBN 978-1-4549-0380-2 (hardcover)
ISBN 978-1-4549-0381-9 (paperback)

Produced by
JR Sansevere

Distributed in Canada by Sterling Publishing
c/o Canadian Manda Group, 165 Dufferin Street
Toronto, Ontario, Canada M6K 3H6
Distributed in the United Kingdom by GMC Distribution Services
Castle Place, 166 High Street, Lewes, East Sussex, England BN7 1XU
Distributed in Australia by Capricorn Link (Australia) Pty. Ltd.
P.O. Box 704, Windsor, NSW 2756, Australia

For information about custom editions, special sales, premium and corporate purchases,
please contact Sterling Special Sales at 800-805-5489 or specialsales@sterlingpublishing.com.

Printed in China

Lot #:
2 4 6 8 10 9 7 5 3 1
11/13

www.sterlingpublishing.com/kids

RICHARD SCARRY'S
Great Big Schoolhouse
Readers

One of the best-selling children's author/illustrators of all time, Richard Scarry has taught generations of children about the world around them—from the alphabet to counting, identifying colors, and even exploring a day at school.

Though Scarry's books are educational, they are beloved for their charming characters, wacky sense of humor, and frenetic energy. Scarry considered himself an entertainer first, and an educator second. He once said, "Everything has an educational value if you look for it. But it's the FUN I want to get across."

A prolific artist, Richard Scarry created more than 300 books, and they have sold over 200 million copies worldwide and have been translated into 30 languages. Richard Scarry died in 1994, but his incredible legacy continues with new books illustrated by his son, Huck Scarry.